JESUS'S TEACHING ON THE LAST DAYS

Understanding the Olivet Discourse in Matthew 24-25

BRYAN HUGHES

TATE PUBLISHING
AND ENTERPRISES, LLC

Published by Tate Publishing & Enterprises, LLC
127 E. Trade Center Terrace | Mustang, Oklahoma 73064 USA
1.888.361.9473 | www.tatepublishing.com

Tate Publishing is committed to excellence in the publishing industry. The company reflects the philosophy established by the founders, based on Psalm 68:11,
"The Lord gave the word and great was the company of those who published it."

Cover design by Samson Lim
Interior design by Gram Telen

Published in the United States of America

ISBN: 978-1-68028-069-2
1. Religion / Biblical Commentary / New Testament
2. Religion / Biblical Biography / New Testament
15.02.21

JESUS'S TEACHING ON THE
LAST DAYS

Acknowledgements

A special thank you to my fellow staff members at Grace Bible Church in Bozeman, MT. It is a privilege to serve with you. Deepest thanks to my wonderful wife, Bev, whose faithful living out of the word of God has always been an example to me.

Contents

Preface

Although this is not a large book and most of the chapters are not very long, there is a lot of information in the pages that follow and some of it is technical in content. Therefore, to get the most out of reading the book, it is recommended that you review the study questions for each chapter listed in the appendix. This will enable the reader to fully grasp the material and avoid confusion. In addition, make sure to read the Bible text noted at the beginning of each chapter and, if possible, read the chapter with your Bible open to the passage being addressed.

In some ways, Jesus's teaching on the last days in the Olivet Discourse is easy to understand and in other ways it is difficult. Therefore, I have sought to present the material in the least-complicated way, which means that I have not gone into nearly as much detail as is possible. However, I hope the reader will find the material sufficient to give clear insight into what Jesus taught.

This discourse was and is one of Jesus's most important sermons. Thus, it is crucial that we seek to understand what He communicated about the future when He spoke these words almost two thousand years ago.

Enjoy!

Introduction

Can you imagine living in a setting where gold is so abundant that silver is about as valuable as common stones and ordinary rocks? There was such a time and it's described in 2nd Chronicles 9. When the Queen of Sheba came to see the wealth and glory of Solomon, what she saw left her breathless. Solomon expanded the kingdom of Israel to its greatest extent ever. Under Solomon, Israel experienced her heyday and her peak. The Queen of Sheba said of Solomon that the half had not been told. He had wealth that you cannot imagine. Twenty-five tons of gold came into the kingdom every year. He had an ivory throne, overlaid with gold. All the furniture and utensils in his palace were overlaid with gold. According to 1st Kings 10:27, he had so much gold that silver was completely worthless; it was like common stones and ordinary rocks. Under his leadership, Israel experienced the golden age. The kingdom was prosperous, broad, safe, secure, and wealthy.

But the crowning achievement of Solomon's kingdom was the temple of God. It stood high in the city of Jerusalem on top of Mt. Moriah. It could be seen for miles, especially when the sun was shining and glistening off the gold and the other shiny building materials. The building began in the spring of 966 BC and it took seven-and-a-half years to complete, which meant that it was finished late in the year 959 BC. There it stood for 373 years until God allowed the Babylonians to capture Jerusalem and to destroy the majestic, beautiful temple. At the same time, the people of Israel were carried away into captivity. But God wasn't finished with His rebellious people. After approximately seventy years of captivity, God allowed the people to return to their land. In 538 BC, a man by the name of Zerubbabel led the first group back to begin rebuilding their temple and their city. This restoration of the temple is described in Ezra 3:8–11. It was a great time in Israel's history. The people had been through a trying and tumultuous time in their lives, and they were finally beginning to get things back together. But some of the older people began weeping because they remembered the magnificence of Solomon's temple and could see that this new temple was going to be much smaller and less glorious. It simply couldn't compare to the beauty or splendor of the first temple. However, it wouldn't remain that way throughout its history. In approximately 19 BC, Herod the Great began a reconstruction and expansion of the temple area, as well as a remodeling of the temple proper. He built a series of retaining walls around the temple and Mt. Moriah, and leveled the top of it. He did this to make the whole complex much larger. And, indeed, it was much larger. The size was staggering. The temple mount or platform was more than one thousand two hundred feet long, which is over four football fields in length, and over eight hundred feet wide. Herod expanded the temple mount to a thirty-five-acre platform. Some of the stones at the base of Herod's temple mount foundation are still in place today near the famous Wailing Wall or Western Wall. One of the rows includes stones that are between eleven to fourteen feet thick and forty-five feet long. A stone with those dimensions would weigh around five hundred seventy metric tons! That is 1.26 million pounds. And those stones aren't even on the bottom row! To this day, no one knows how Herod's builders got those stones into place, fitting them together with such precision that you can't even slip a credit card between them. It was an engineering feat that is probably unequaled.

Herod began this reconstruction, expansion, and remodeling project around 19 BC. By the time Jesus and His disciples were in Jerusalem at the end of Jesus's life, the project would have been going on almost fifty years. You can't imagine how magnificent the temple complex was by that time. It was a spectacle to behold. With massive stone blocks decorated with gold ornamentation, Herod's temple was, without a doubt, one of the most impressive structures in the world. Yet, it also would be destroyed, just as Solomon's temple was. In AD 70, the destruction would come from the hands of the Romans. Jesus knew it was coming some forty years before it actually happened. But He knew more than that. He knew what was going to happen in the last days of life as we know it on planet earth. One day as He sat with His disciples on the Mount of Olives, He revealed to them many of those future events. Matthew recorded that teaching of Jesus and included it in chapters 24–25 of his gospel. So, we have the opportunity and privilege to read Jesus's teaching on the last days.

1

The Destruction of the Temple

Matthew 24:1–2

The final verses of Matthew 23 record the lament of Jesus over the city of Jerusalem. Because the people were blindly following their religious leaders and because they would not heed the invitations of Jesus to come to Him for salvation, the judgment of God was headed their way. When Jesus left the temple for this final time, it was no longer God's house. Because the nation as a whole rejected their Messiah, God's presence departed and He left His house to the people of Israel. It was now just an empty shell. The people of Israel would continue their sacrifices and rituals in that place for the next forty years until God finally put an end to it with His judgment through the Romans in AD 70. That's what Jesus warned about in the opening verses of chapter 24.

His warning was prompted by the action of the disciples when they pointed out the spectacular buildings among the temple complex. Jesus had seen those temple buildings many times in His life. So, it seems that the disciples were asking Jesus a question without asking Him a question. When they heard Jesus say, "Behold! Your house is left to you desolate," in Matthew 23:38, they knew He was saying something ominous about the temple. They didn't know all that Jesus meant by that statement, but they knew it wasn't good. So, they were basically asking Jesus for more information regarding what all was involved in His statement. The disciples couldn't imagine how this magnificent structure could be desolate. Knowing that they were wondering about these things, Jesus responded with a startling prediction of the coming destruction of the temple. In AD 70, a general named Titus led his Roman army of approximately eighty thousand troops to the city of Jerusalem. They destroyed the city and the temple. Still to this day you can see some of the large stones they threw down from the temple mount because those stones are sitting down at the bottom of the southwest corner. Not only were the city and temple destroyed, the people were massacred. The Roman army killed approximately one million one hundred thousand Jewish men, women, and children and threw their bodies over the walls of the city.

In the gospel records, we are only told about Jesus crying on two occasions. One of them is found in John 11 when He came to the tomb of His friend, Lazarus. The other time was when He thought about the coming destruction of Jerusalem. It's recorded in Luke 19:41–42, where we are given a glimpse of the great compassion of Jesus. His heart was broken because the Jews rejected His salvation. They were so busy with their religion that they didn't have time for Jesus, Himself. In Luke 13:34, He said to Jerusalem, "How often I wanted to gather your children together as a hen gathers her brood under her wings, but you were not willing!" (NKJV) Because they were not willing, they experienced the judgment of God.

However, even the events of AD 70 would not be the last time the Jewish people would encounter extreme adversity. Jesus taught that another time is coming in which the Jewish people will face tribulation unlike anything they have ever experienced in their history.

2

The Olivet Discourse

Matthew 24:3

Beginning in Matthew 24:3, we have the final extended discourse of our Lord recorded in the Gospel of Matthew. This is one of the most controversial sections in Matthew's entire gospel. The proposed interpretations of these passages are quite diverse. Often the disagreements center on the issue of eschatology. Eschatology is the technical term for a person's view of the end times or the last days. This discourse is a key passage for that topic of theology. There are some who say that this chapter doesn't have any bearing on eschatology because they say that the events of this chapter were all fulfilled in AD 70 when the Romans destroyed Jerusalem and the temple. Others say that this discourse by Jesus goes well beyond AD 70, and it addresses events that will take place in the last days. Because there are these differences of opinion and because this can be a difficult section of Scripture to understand, we will devote this chapter to an overview of the entire discourse, before looking at the details in the following chapters.

The Olivet Discourse, which is the technical title for this section, begins in verse 4 and goes all the way to the end of chapter 25. There is a chapter break in our English Bibles, but the discourse is actually one unit. Therefore, it is important that we understand the judgment of the sheep and goats at the end of chapter 25, in connection with what Jesus says in chapter 24. Many Christians do not do that. They pull the sheep and goat judgment out of its context and end up teachings things that Jesus was not intending to teach. Some use it to teach works salvation and some use it to teach that every Christian ought to be involved in specific kinds of ministry but, in the context, Jesus wasn't really teaching any of those things. It's good to be involved in prison ministry or hospital ministry or feeding the poor ministry if the Lord directs you that way, but that is not really the point of what Jesus was saying when He talked about the sheep and goat judgment. The passage must be understood in the context of the entire discourse.

Jesus gave this discourse to answer a question from the disciples that was prompted by what He had said regarding the desolation and destruction of the temple. In Matthew 23:38, Jesus had told the religious leaders of His day that the temple was no longer God's house. When Jesus departed from the temple, in verse 1 of chapter 24, the glory of God departed from the temple and it was left desolate. It sat abandoned by God for almost forty years, even though the Jewish people were oblivious to the fact that God was no longer there. They continued to go to the temple and offer sacrifices, but it was all a bunch of meaningless liturgy. God had moved out. After forty years of these continual sacrifices, which were an affront to the Lord's perfect and final sacrifice on the cross, God's patience had reached its end. Not only would the temple be left desolate, it would be destroyed. Jesus predicted that in verses 1–2 of this 24th chapter.

This made no sense to the disciples whatsoever. They knew that the nation of Israel was God's chosen nation. They knew that Jerusalem was God's chosen city. They knew that the temple was God's house. They had become convinced that Jesus was God's Messiah, the king of Israel. So, in their minds, they figured that Jesus would establish the kingdom promised for Israel throughout Hebrew Scripture. They assumed that He would exalt Jerusalem, so that the temple would become the worship center for the entire world but, instead, Jesus predicted the desolation and destruction of the temple. So, the disciples asked Jesus to tell them when these things would come to pass and what would be the sign of His coming and the end of the age. It's important to realize the disciples didn't know about a second coming of Jesus. At this point, they still didn't understand that Jesus was going to die and go away. So when they asked these questions, they weren't asking about His second coming. They were simply asking Jesus when He was going to come forward as the Messiah, the king of Israel, and end the present age by bringing in the kingdom age. They actually asked two questions because they probably assumed they were basically the same question. First, they asked, "When will these things be?" Then they asked, "And what will be the sign of Your coming, and of the end of the age?" What they didn't realize was that the two questions were separate issues because the destruction of the temple would take place in AD 70, but the end of the age would come much later. They almost certainly assumed that the two were connected in some way and would be at the same time. In fact, they probably thought the two events were going to happen at any moment. Luke 19:11 tells us that because Jesus was in Jerusalem, the disciples thought the kingdom of God would appear immediately. So they asked Jesus for clarification. The Olivet Discourse is His answer.

In Matthew's account of this discourse, Jesus didn't give the disciples a lot of specifics concerning the destruction of Jerusalem and the temple in AD 70, but He did give them a lot of information about His coming and the end of the age. Jesus began by telling them about the events leading up to His coming and the end of the age. In verses 4–8, He describes the first half of the future tribulation period and in verses 9 and following He describes the second half of the future tribulation period.

How do we know that Jesus is describing the future tribulation period in these verses? There are three reasons: (1) Because Jesus says in verse 8 that "these are the beginning of sorrows" or "the beginning of birth pangs." In other words, when these things begin to happen with more frequency and intensity, that is an indication that something big is about to happen. When a woman begins to experience frequent and intense labor pains, that is a sign that the baby is coming. When this world begins to experience the events in verses 4–7 with frequency and intensity, that is a sign that Jesus is coming. (2) Because in verse 15, Jesus makes mention of the abomination of desolation. That phrase comes out of Daniel 9, where the context is God's final dealings with the people of Israel "to bring in everlasting righteousness" (Daniel 9:24). This fits with what Paul says in 2nd Thessalonians 2:4 regarding the future man of sin, or Antichrist, who will set himself up in the temple to demand worship as God. This is confirmed in Revelation

13:14–15 as a future event. We know from Daniel 9:27 that this future event known as "the abomination of desolation" will take place at the midpoint of the seven-year tribulation. (3) Because in verse 29, Jesus specifically declared that He was describing a future tribulation that would be followed by His second coming from heaven. So, for those three reasons, we know that this discourse by Jesus pertains to the future seven-year tribulation period.

There is another important feature of this discourse to keep in mind, and that is the fact that it focuses on the Jewish people. A failure to recognize this will result in a lot of confusion. Remember, it was prompted by questions that the disciples asked when Jesus predicted the destruction of the temple in verses 1–2. Furthermore, in verse 15, Jesus said a key event in this time period will be the abomination of desolation in the temple. That is a Jewish issue, not Gentile, and it is confirmed by the mention of Judea in verse 16. A failure to understand the Jewish focus of this discourse is how so many Christians get confused when they read it. They read these words as if Jesus was speaking to the church, but the church isn't the focus of this discourse—the Jewish people are the focus of this discourse. That is further reinforced in verse 20 when Jesus refers to the travel restrictions on the Sabbath. What difference would it make if Christians around the world had to flee persecution on a Saturday? None. So the comments about the temple, the comments about Judea, and the comments about the Sabbath make it clear that the nation of Israel is the focus of this discourse.

This sermon by Jesus culminates in a description of His second coming to the earth in 24:29–31. After Jesus mentions His second coming in those verses, He elaborates on it by giving a series of parables or illustrations in the verses that follow. In verses 32–35, He gives the parable of the fig tree. In verses 36–44, He illustrates the similarities with the days of Noah. In verses 45–51, He drives home the point by telling the story of the two servants. In the first 13 verses of chapter 25, He tells the parable of the ten virgins. In verses 14–30, He tells the parable of the talents. In 25:31, He reiterates His future coming in glory to judge the nations in the sheep and goat judgment. All of those stories relate to His second coming, which is the culmination of this Olivet Discourse.

One other key observation about this discourse is that Jesus indicates that all these events will lead to a future kingdom. In 25:31, Jesus began to describe the sheep and goat judgment. That will take place after the seven-year tribulation period and after the second coming of the Lord Jesus to the earth, but it will be before or at the beginning of the kingdom that Jesus comes to establish. All the Gentiles who are alive after the second coming will be gathered before Jesus at the judgment of the sheep and goats. They will be judged based upon how they treated the Jewish brethren of Jesus during their intense time of persecution throughout the seven-year tribulation period. Why will that be the basis? Because a person's true spiritual condition of salvation or condemnation will be manifested in how that person related to the persecuted Jewish people throughout the tribulation period. Only those who truly know and love the Lord Jesus will be willing to come to the aid of the Jewish people during that time because the Jewish people will be hated by everyone else (24:9). So, if a person is willing to help the Jewish people, you can be confident that such an individual had truly received the Lord Jesus as his personal Lord and savior. It's not that an individual will earn his salvation by ministering to the Jewish people. He will simply prove or verify or manifest the genuineness of his salvation in that way. Those who end up demonstrating the reality of their salvation in that way will be welcomed into the kingdom. Those who prove by their actions that they are goats and not sheep will be excluded from the kingdom. So it is clear that when Jesus returns to this earth at the end of the tribulation period, He is coming to establish the kingdom. Finally, the prayer of God's people down through the centuries, "Thy kingdom come," will be answered.

We wouldn't know from this passage how long the earthly kingdom lasts, but we are told in Revelation 20 that it will last a thousand years. That's why it is often referred to as the millennial kingdom, since the word *millennium* means one thousand. Six specific times the phrase "thousand years" is used in Revelation 20 to describe the future earthly kingdom. When God says something that many times, there is no excuse for us not hearing what He has said. The future earthly kingdom that was promised throughout Hebrew Scripture will last a thousand years and that will lead into the eternal heavenly kingdom.

It is quite powerful to think about Jesus sitting on the Mount of Olives, overlooking the city of Jerusalem and the majestic temple, speaking these words about the future of the Jewish people. He knew that they were going to experience a time of horrendous judgment in AD 70 when the Romans came sweeping through as the rod of God's judgment. He also knew that the Jewish people will someday experience another horrific time of persecution and judgment during the future tribulation period, but it will lead to the glorious kingdom of Messiah Jesus.

3

The Beginning of Birth Pains

Matthew 24:4–8

Childbirth is an amazing experience. I had the privilege of being present for the births of all three of our children, and it probably wouldn't be an overstatement to say that it is a miraculous event. What was also miraculous was that I didn't pass out in the delivery room! But that's another story. It is remarkable that a little human being can live inside his mother and then come forth to the outside world. What is also fascinating to consider is that a nine-month pregnant mother can sometimes go along in life with very little hint that labor is about to begin until it actually begins. Other times there are numerous hints along the way. Sometimes the labor begins slowly, before building to the intensity of the actual birth. That is the imagery our Lord uses in Matthew 24 to describe the future tribulation period

Verses 4–8 are the first part of the Olivet Discourse given by Jesus in Matthew's Gospel. It is not surprising that Matthew recorded this sermon by Jesus. Matthew's Gospel account is more Jewish in its content than any of the others. It was written by a Jewish man to the Jewish people to convince them of their Jewish Messiah, Jesus. So, it shouldn't surprise us that Matthew would make sure to record this message, explaining what is going to happen to the Jewish people at the end of the age. The focus of the discourse is God's program for the Jewish people in the last days and leading into the kingdom age. The events that our Lord mentioned in verses 4–8 are called the beginning of birth pains or the beginning of sorrows. The future tribulation period is going to be a time of pain and sorrow for the Jewish people who are alive on planet earth at that time. They will be hated, persecuted, and killed; but eventually they will be converted and delivered. So, the word *picture* used by Jesus when He used the phrase "the beginning of birth pains" is a very accurate description. The process will not be pleasant, by any means, but the end result will be wonderful.

Even though this discourse by Jesus emphasizes the Jewish struggles at the end of the age, it would be wrong to assume that nothing is going to be happening in the lives of others in the world at the time. The book of Revelation makes it clear that many things will be happening all over the face of the planet and in the lives of all the people who will be living at that time. Revelation 6–18 tells us a great deal about those events. Just as John's Gospel spends over half the book describing the final week of Jesus's life, so also John spends over half the book of Revelation describing the final week of years foretold in Daniel's great prophecy of Daniel 9. At the end of Daniel 9, the angel Gabriel told Daniel that God would focus on Israel for a period of four hundred ninety years, and when that time period is all over, it will cause Israel's rebellion to cease. At the end of this four hundred ninety-year period, Israel will no longer be in rebellion, and the result will be everlasting righteousness. Four hundred and eighty three years of that time have already elapsed. That leaves a period of seven years. According to Daniel 9:27, that final seven-year period will begin when the prince who is to come (the Antichrist) makes some kind of treaty with Israel. But, after three-and-a-half years, he will break that treaty. He will not allow the Jewish people to carry out their sacrifices and, according to 2nd Thessalonians and Revelation, he will demand that they worship him. Because the people of Israel will refuse, he will begin to persecute them ruthlessly. That seven-year time period is what is described for us in Revelation 6–18. The first eight verses of Revelation 6 describe the beginning of sorrows, to use the phrase Jesus used in Matthew 24.

By comparing the description of the first four seals of Revelation 6 with Jesus's words in Matthew 24, we understand that both passages describe the first three-and-a-half years of the seven-year tribulation period. Both passages emphasize that deception will reign throughout those years. That is why Jesus said not to be deceived. The Antichrist will deceive multitudes, and the false prophet will deceive just as many, and maybe even more. But even prior to or along with those dominant characters of the end times, there will be many people proclaiming themselves as the one who can solve the problems of the world. They will proclaim themselves as the answer to man's problems. They will claim to be Christ, and many will believe them. The last days will start out peaceful but end up being characterized by war and disaster. Both Matthew 24 and Revelation 6 record that same message. In addition, famine will run rampant in the end times. All of these tragedies result in massive death, which is emphasized by Jesus in Matthew 24 and John in Revelation 6. The parallels are clear and obvious because Jesus's words in the Olivet Discourse and Revelation 6 are describing the same time period of the future. The book of Revelation emphasizes the global scale of these events, whereas Jesus (in Matthew 24) is more focused on how these things will affect the Jewish people. But both passages are describing the same time period. Jesus compared this time to the birth pangs of a woman in labor. They start out slow and with less intensity, but they increase in rapidity and intensity. That's the way the seven-year tribulation period will unfold. It will start out peaceful, but then the birth pangs will begin as seals two, three, and four in Revelation 6 are opened.

Jesus doesn't give all the same details that are recorded in Revelation 6–18 because, as has been noted, His focus is on how these events will affect the Jewish people. That is why His emphasis, in verses 9–26, is on how the Jewish people are going to be hated and how they are going to be persecuted.

4

Hated by All Nations

Matthew 24:9–14

One of the many things that is so amazing about the Bible is the fact that, although written hundreds and thousands of years ago, it is more current and relevant than anything being written today. Not only that, it will continue to be relevant tomorrow and the day after, the week after, the month after, and the year after, until Jesus comes back. That is because it is not merely the word of man; it is the inspired word of God. It's not a dead book. Hebrews 4:12 says, "For the word of God is living and powerful, and sharper than any two-edged sword, piercing even to the division of soul and spirit, and of joints and marrow, and is a discerner of the thoughts and intents of the heart." Because the Bible is the Word of God, it is eternally relevant. It is more than relevant; it is ahead of its time. It speaks to the issues of our day, and it even speaks to the issues that will come about in this world in the future. God writes history in advance. He tells what is going to happen to people, to cities, to kingdoms, and ultimately what is going to happen in this world. When He does, He makes sure that it is written down so that there is no confusion or misunderstanding or no backing away from what has been said. That is exactly what we find in the Olivet Discourse recorded in Matthew 24–25.

This section of Scripture is futuristic in its focus. It gives information about what is coming in the future days during the end times. It is intended to be read by the people who will be living at the end of the age. We know that by the statement at the end of verse 15, "whoever reads, let him understand." Those words were either spoken by Jesus because He knew this would be read by people in the end times, or it was written by Matthew under the inspiration of the Holy Spirit for the same reason. Either way, it shows us that even though Jesus spoke these words to His disciples, they would not be the ones experiencing these things. These events will take place in the future near the end of the age.

Throughout verses 9–14, Jesus mentions persecution that will come upon the Jewish people. So, it is obvious that the Jewish people are the target group for this teaching by Jesus. Since the focus is on events in the end times, we can conclude that these words were recorded to be read by the Jewish people living at that time. They will be the ones who will experience the persecution that is described in verses 9–14. They are the "you" spoken of throughout the passage. They are the ones who "will be hated by all nations." Not only that, during the future tribulation period, Satan and the Antichrist will unleash all of their fury on the Jewish people. This fact is depicted in Revelation chapter 12.

When you look back over the last sixty-seven years, it really is miraculous that Israel still exists. In May of 1948 the British withdrew from Palestine. On May 14, 1948, Israel declared her independence. On the same day, five Arab armies invaded the State of Israel to destroy her. That precipitated the War of Independence and, amazingly, when all the dust settled, Israel had gained more territory than she would have received in the United Nations Partition Plan developed in November of 1947. Then, in June of 1967, there was the Six-Day War with Egypt, Syria, and Jordan. Israel conquered Sinai again, including Gaza, the Golan Heights, and the West Bank. Then, in October of 1973, Israel fought the Yom Kippur War. It came about due to a surprise attack in Sinai by Egypt and in the Golan Heights by Syria. Israel was completely unprepared and, for a while, her existence was hanging in the balance. Still today it is the stated intention of many of Israel's neighbors to push her out into the Mediterranean Sea and eliminate her existence. Yet, Israel remains. And she will continue to exist because God has future plans for that tiny, but extremely significant, nation. We are told this time and again in the pages of predictive prophecy.

Israel is still in existence today but, because she still hasn't embraced Messiah Jesus, she is going to go through a time of immense suffering. There's no question that the Jewish people have suffered down through the centuries, but their worst suffering is yet to come. However, God will not allow them to be annihilated. That's what Jesus stated in Matthew 24:22 and that's what the Apostle John described in Revelation 12:13–17. God will not allow them to be annihilated because He has committed Himself to bringing them to salvation and to a place of blessing again in the future. Israel has not been in that place for thousands of years. The people of Israel are not at the center of God's saving program now because "the fullness of the Gentiles" (Romans 11:25) has not yet been fulfilled. And the capital city of Israel, which is Jerusalem, does not occupy the place of prominence that it will one day have under Christ, because now it is under the "times of the Gentiles" (Luke 21:24). Once the "fullness of the Gentiles has come in," that is, once God has saved all the Gentiles He has purposed to save, God will turn back to Israel to begin ending the times of the Gentiles. But Satan will try to thwart God's plan. According to what Jesus says in Mathew 24 and what John says in Revelation 12, during the tribulation period Satan will attempt to destroy Israel. Zechariah 13:8 indicates that two-thirds of the Jewish population will die during this time. In Matthew 24:21, Jesus said, "For then shall be great tribulation, such as was not since the beginning of the world to this time, no, nor ever shall be." There will be satanic persecution, natural catastrophes, unprecedented demonic activity, and much of it will be directed against Israel. That's why Jeremiah 30:7 says it will be "the time of Jacob's trouble." But God will protect and preserve the nation to save them. In Zechariah 13:9 God says, "I will bring the one-third through the fire, Will refine them as silver is refined, and test them as gold is tested; They will call on My name, and I will answer them. I will say, 'This is my people'; and each one will say, 'The Lord is my God.'" God will use the intense suffering of Israel to bring the people to repentance. He is just as committed to fulfilling His purposes with them as He has ever been. Jesus doesn't give all the details in Matthew 24, but He does give an overview.

Jesus warned that the Jewish people will be hated by all nations at that time. Why? One possibility is that the Gentile nations may assume that Israel is somehow responsible for all the catastrophes that are taking place on the earth, as described in the first four seal judgments of Revelation 6. Whatever the excuse, the nations of the world are going to find a reason to hate and persecute and kill the Jewish people. Not only that, it is possible that some within the Jewish community will even betray each other. When this kind of chaos comes about, people start looking for help, answers, or solutions. That makes them vulnerable to people who step forward and claim to have a word from God or claim to be a spokesman for God. So, Jesus warned about massive deception during the last days. Satan knows that God's plan is to bring the people of Israel to repentance and to faith in Messiah Jesus. But Satan doesn't want that. So he is going to throw as many false prophets at them as he can in an attempt to deceive them and mislead them. And he will succeed in large measure. Jesus warned that many will be deceived. Many will be deceived by the Antichrist, the false prophet of Revelation 13, and the multitude of false prophets that will proliferate the scene of the end times. Not only will many be deceived, many will become so desperate in the midst of the chaos and anarchy that they will be willing to turn on each other and betray the very ones they ought to love. The events of the end times will be so chaotic that some parts of the world will be reduced to anarchy.

Unless you have lived through such a scenario, you can't appreciate how awful that kind of situation really is. I once had a conversation with a missionary in Albania, who told me about a time when he and his family lived through anarchy in that country. The governmental structure collapsed and, as a result, there was no police and no protection in place for people. He told me about things that were horrific. That's what happens in a time of lawlessness and anarchy. His closing statement was, "A bad government is way better than no government at all. You don't want be in a place where there is lawlessness and anarchy." When that happens, the true nature of much of humanity comes out. When people can do whatever they want and get away with it, the result is unspeakable. The supposed love that people have for one another becomes nonexistent, as Jesus warned about in His sermon.

However, there will be those who survive to the end and who remain faithful to the Lord God and they will be delivered from the horrors of the tribulation to enter into the glorious kingdom that will be brought by the Lord Jesus in His second coming. God is going to make sure that all the nations of the world hear the gospel before this age comes to an end. Jesus stated that the gospel of the kingdom will be preached in all the world. The word *gospel* means good news. So the gospel of the kingdom is the good news of the kingdom. According to verse 29, "immediately after the tribulation," Jesus is going to return to this earth. He is coming back to bring in the literal, earthly kingdom. That will be good news to those who are in the tribulation period and don't want to commit themselves to the Antichrist and his kingdom. Many of the people on the planet at the time will reject this good news and they will take the mark of the beast. But some will hear the gospel or good news of the kingdom and will embrace Jesus, regardless of the price they have to pay. God is going to make sure that this opportunity is given throughout the world to all the nations, and then the end will come.

5

The Abomination that Causes Desolation

Matthew 24:15

One of the most photographed locations in our world today is the ancient temple mount in Jerusalem, taken from the Mount of Olives on the east side of Jerusalem. Who hasn't seen a picture of that golden Dome of the Rock that dominates the landscape of Jerusalem? Although many people have seen a picture of that mosque, very few know how it got there.

In approximately 63 BC, the Roman Empire conquered the world and was in power during the New Testament era. The Jewish people were in the land of Israel at that time, but they and the land were basically controlled by Rome. Needless to say, the Jewish people didn't like being controlled and dominated by the Roman Empire. So, from time to time, they would resist and carry out revolt. In AD 66, over thirty years after Jesus had died, resurrected, and ascended, Rome decided to stamp out Jewish rebellion in

Israel once and for all. They started in the northern part of Israel, in Galilee, then on to Samaria, Peraea, and Idumea. It took over two years to successfully carry out these operations. Then, in AD 70, Vespasian, the Roman emperor, decided to go after Jerusalem. After weeks of assault, Jerusalem fell. The temple was burned and destroyed on the 9th of Av (about August 28) in that year.

Fast forward about five hundred years to AD 570. That was the year Muhammad was born in Mecca, Arabia. Muhammad was the founder of Islam. In time, he was able to establish a theocratic Muslim state that soon engulfed all of Arabia and large parts of North Africa and Western Asia. Shortly after his death, the city of Jerusalem was captured in AD 638. Fifty-three years after that, in AD 691, the famous Dome of the Rock was built on the sight of the ancient temple mount.

The Dome of the Rock is built over the spot where Muslims believe Muhammad ascended in the night on a journey to heaven. According to Islamic teaching, that makes Jerusalem their third holiest site in the world, just behind Mecca and Medina. There are actually two mosques on top of the temple mount. There is the Dome of the Rock, which is somewhat centrally located, and there is the Al-Aqsa Mosque on the southern end of the ancient temple mount. That is the mosque in which Muslims worship today because the Dome of the Rock is primarily just a monument to Islam. So, two mosques sit on top of the ancient temple mount.

However, the day is coming when there will be another Jewish temple on top of that site. The word of God is clear on that fact. We don't know exactly where it will be located, but we do know that there will be another temple there someday. In fact, there is a group in Jerusalem right now, called the Third Temple Treasury, that has made all the garments and all the implements necessary to have a functioning temple. They are located in the Jewish Quarter of the Old City. Whether they are the group to build the third temple or not, there will be another Jewish temple on the temple mount someday. This reality is indicated in Daniel 9, Matthew 24, 2nd Thessalonians 2, and Revelation 11.

In Revelation 11:1, the Apostle John was instructed to measure the temple he saw in his vision. It may be that John was instructed to do this so that he would know for sure that this temple he was measuring was not the same one that was destroyed in AD 70 by the Romans. Revelation 11 describes a different temple, the one that will exist in the tribulation period. So, there will be a temple and the Jews will worship in that temple until the abomination of desolation. Then everything will change. That's what Jesus warned about in Matthew 24:15.

In the early verses of Matthew 24, Jesus stated that the Jewish people will be hated and persecuted. The key event in connection with their persecution will be the abomination of desolation. That phrase actually comes out of Daniel 9:27, which teaches that a future prince or leader will sign a seven-year covenant, but he will break that covenant in the middle. Part of his breaking of the covenant will involve his decision to bring an end to sacrifice and offering. Therefore, it's possible that the covenant initially involved permission for the Jewish people to rebuild their temple and resume their sacrifices. But that will be halted at the midpoint of the seven years in the event known as the abomination of desolation.

Daniel 7:25 tells us that this future ruler will blaspheme God, wage war against the saints, and try to change the times and laws. In 2nd Thessalonians 2:4, Paul says he "opposes and exalts himself above all that is called God or that is worshiped, so that he sits as God in the temple of God, showing himself that he is God." Daniel 11:36 says that this king will "do according to his own will." In other words, he will do whatever he wants to do and all of it is evil, which is why 2nd Thessalonians 2:3 calls him "the man of sin." He will eventually demand that everyone in the world take his mark, as seen in Revelation 13. It seems that these atrocities flow from this one, key event called the abomination of desolation.

The Jewish people will face their worst persecution ever when the Antichrist sets up in the temple the abomination that makes desolate. And God will use that persecution to finally bring His chosen people to repentance, so they will embrace their Messiah, Jesus. That's what it will take to get them to repent and believe in Jesus.

6

Then There Will Be Great Tribulation

Matthew 24:16

It is a fact of history that the Jewish people have suffered immensely. The most notable occasion was the holocaust of the last century, but there have been many other occasions throughout history in various places around the world. Because anti-Semitism is rampant in our world and because Satan hates God's chosen people, the Jews have been the brunt of many forms of persecution down through the centuries. But, amazingly, their greatest suffering is yet to come. There are many passages in Scripture that predict this fact and one of them records the words of Jesus Himself on the subject. It is Matthew 24.

These words, although spoken to the disciples, are intended for the Jewish people who will be living during the future tribulation period. We know that because of the parenthetical comment at the end of verse 15, which says, "whoever reads, let him understand." Some of the Jewish people will read these words during the tribulation period and they will know what to do.

Jesus told His disciples what is going to happen with and to the Jewish people at the end of the age. They will be hated and they will be persecuted. The key event in connection with their persecution will be the abomination of desolation spoken of by Jesus in verse 15. What Jesus didn't mention in that verse is who it is that will commit the abomination of desolation. That's probably because the book of Daniel spells that out in such detail that Jesus didn't feel the need to elaborate any further. The book of Daniel tells us that there will arise a man in the future who will become the leader of the world. He is called by various titles in Scripture but we know him most commonly as the Antichrist. He is such a dominant figure in Scripture that 1st John 2:18 says, "Little children. . . you have heard that the Antichrist is coming." John's readers had heard about this man because he's mentioned many times throughout the Scripture. He is described in great detail in 2nd Thessalonians 2 and Revelation 13. He is the one who will commit the abomination of desolation. When he does, Jesus warned the people of Israel to flee. He specifically mentioned those living in Judea, which is the southern part of the land of Israel. That's where the city of Jerusalem is located. That's where the first two temples stood and that is where the third temple will someday stand. There, the Antichrist will commit the abomination of desolation by setting up himself or an image of himself in the temple and will demand that the Jews worship him. When they refuse, he will persecute them ruthlessly. That's why Jesus warned those in Judea to flee to the mountains. Because of their proximity to Jerusalem, they will be the first to come under the Antichrist's wrath.

There is a mountainous region southeast of Jerusalem, around the Dead Sea, that has lots of caves and places to hide. That's where David hid from Saul and that area may be where the Jews initially flee when the persecution breaks out. In addition, there are a number of mountainous regions in the hills of Moab and Edom. The Jewish people are going to need all the places of refuge they can find because the Antichrist's fury will be the most intense persecution ever as he tries to annihilate the Jewish people.

7

Israel's Flight from Antichrist

Matthew 24:17–22

The day is coming when a man is going to walk this planet, unlike any other man who has ever existed. From the standpoint of resistance to God and His plan, he will be the consummate man. He will be Satan's man. Just as the Lord Jesus Christ perfectly fulfilled the will of the Father, so also will the Antichrist perfectly fulfill the will of Satan. There have been several men in history who had some of the characteristics this man will have. Like Hitler, he will hate and persecute the Jews. Like Nebuchadnezzar, he will rule the world. But there were two other men in history who uniquely picture for us what the Antichrist will be like. Those two men were Antiochus Epiphanes and Alexander the Great. They foreshadowed the coming Antichrist. Antiochus Epiphanes is a picture of the evil character of the Antichrist, whereas Alexander the Great is a picture of the military and administrative genius of the coming Antichrist. It's interesting that both of those men are prominent in the book of Daniel and both of them point to the Antichrist, who will be a combination of their lives, plus much more. The Antichrist will be the ultimate man but not in a positive way. He will be: (1) an intellectual genius. Daniel 7:8 says he will have "eyes like the eyes of a man." Eyes are used in apocalyptic passages to speak of intelligence. (2) an outstanding orator. Daniel 7:8 also says that he will have "a mouth speaking pompous words." He will have a commanding personality and he will be a very charismatic leader. (3) a military genius. Daniel 7:23 says he "shall devour the whole earth, trample it and break it in pieces." And after he breaks his covenant with Israel, he will begin to persecute them with all the hatred of Antiochus Epiphanes and more.

In verses 16–22 of Matthew 24, Jesus taught that the Jewish people are going to be the target of the Antichrist's wrath during the last days. Therefore, when they see the abomination of desolation take place in the temple, Jesus told them to flee. The persecution is going to be so severe that the Jewish people, especially those in Judea, shouldn't even take the time to gather their belongings to flee. Just get out of there! Time is of the essence. The Jewish people are quickly going to become the focus of the Antichrist's wrath and fury. Jesus warned that it will be especially difficult for those who are pregnant or nursing. Those circumstances will make it difficult to flee in haste. In addition, Jesus also mentioned the difficulty that would accompany the situation if these events unfold in winter or on the Sabbath. Both of those situations would slow down travel for the Jewish people. The winter is the rainy season in Israel and the Sabbath Day, which is Saturday, is a day when many services, such as buses and trains, are curtailed. So, if the abomination of desolation takes place in the winter or on a Saturday, then that will really slow things down for the Jewish people who are attempting to flee. But regardless of the conditions or circumstances, one thing is certain and that is the fact that the Jewish people will need to do everything they can as soon as they can to escape the Antichrist's attempts to annihilate them. Because that is exactly what he is going to try to do. Jesus made the startling announcement in verse 21: "For then there will be tribulation, such as has not been since the beginning of the world until this time, no, nor ever shall be." That is an astounding statement when you stop to realize just how much tribulation the Jewish people have experienced down through the centuries. They have experienced so much tribulation and persecution simply because they are Jewish. The most notable example is the holocaust but there are many others. Yet, Jesus said that what they will face in the future will exceed all that they have experienced in the past. He calls it "great tribulation." That is the phrase we often use to distinguish the second half of the seven-year tribulation period. The whole time will be a time of tribulation in various ways, but the last half will be the great tribulation. Revelation 6–18 informs us why it is called that. Those chapters record all the cataclysmic events that will be taking place on planet earth, in addition to the persecution that will be directed at the Jewish people. Jeremiah 30:7 refers to it as the time of Jacob's trouble.

However, God will not let this persecution go on indefinitely. He will restrict it for the elect's sake. The Antichrist will only be allowed to carry out his heinous intentions for the final three and a half years of the tribulation period. Then Jesus will return to stop the bloodbath and will execute His own judgment.

The *elect* in verse 22 is a reference to the Jewish people. They were the ones chosen in the book of Genesis to be the people in whom and through whom God worked to bless the world. They have blessed the world beyond description because they are the ones God used to give us His word and His Son. The Scripture came through the Jewish people, and the Lord Jesus came through the Jewish people. And because God chose them, He gave them unconditional promises that are still going to be fulfilled in the future. They are going to receive the glorious kingdom that was promised to them throughout Hebrew Scripture. But that raises a question when we read what Jesus said in Matthew 24. Why is the Lord going to allow all of this to take place? Why is He going to allow His chosen people to experience such atrocities? Because that is what it will take to finally bring about their salvation. Their own prophets often referred to them as a stubborn and stiff-necked people. They won't repent of their ways, and they won't embrace Jesus as their Messiah. So God will allow all of this to take place to bring them to the point where they will finally look to Jesus as their Messiah.

8

Warnings about False Messiahs

Matthew 24:23–28

People in our world are fascinated with knowing the future. It has always been that way. People spend enormous amounts of money going to fortune tellers, mediums, spiritists, and witches to try to find out what is going to happen in the future. Sometimes those fortune tellers get a few things right because, after all, even a stopped clock is right two times every twenty-four hours. But when God tells the future, He is always 100 percent accurate. Not only that but He writes it down so everyone can see and know exactly what He has said and so that everyone can verify the accuracy of what He has said, once the event has taken place. A perfect example of this is Matthew 24. There, Jesus foretold the future and Matthew recorded it under the inspiration of the Holy Spirit for all to read, especially those who will be living when the events take place.

In verses 16–22 of Matthew 24, Jesus warned about Satan's future attempts to destroy the Jewish people physically. In verses 23–28, He warned about Satan's future attempts to destroy them spiritually by getting them to believe in a false Christ. Understandably, when the Jewish people are going through all these horrors, they will want someone to step forward to be their savior, and Satan will use that in an attempt to deceive them to believe in a false Christ. It will be very easy for the Jewish people to believe in those false christs because they will be grasping at whoever promises them protection and deliverance. Twice in this passage Jesus sternly warned, "Do not believe it." Not only will the terrible circumstances make it easy for the Jewish people to be deceived, Jesus also announced that the false christs and false prophets will be able to show great signs and wonders. That will make the false christs extremely believable. They will be satanically enabled to perform miracles and great signs. Second Thessalonians 2:9 says, "The coming of the lawless one is according to the working of Satan, with all power, signs, and lying wonders." Those three words used there in that verse (power or miracles, signs, and wonders) are the exact same three words used in Acts 2:22 to describe the miracles of Jesus and the same three words used in Hebrews 2:4 to describe the miracles of the apostles. These will not be mere *tricks* or *gimmicks*. They will be miracles. So, the false prophet of Revelation 13 will not be the only one who will do miracles during this time. The Antichrist himself will also be able to do them, as well as other false christs. Satan knows how gullible many people are when they believe everything that is miraculous is automatically of God. That's what many Christians even believe today, which is why there is so much error under the umbrella of Christianity. Ever since his fall, Satan has been a counterfeiter. He seeks to counterfeit God in every way imaginable. The Lord God has His Christ, so Satan has his

Antichrist. The apostles of Jesus used signs to point people to the Lord Jesus, so the false prophet will use signs to point people to the Antichrist. And tragically, many people will fall for this deception.

When you stop to think about it, Jesus was very gracious to give this warning in advance. He knew what is coming and that is why He gives this teaching. He realized that when all of this chaos and catastrophe begins to break out, many of the Jewish people are going to start reading the Gospel of Matthew. That is indicated in the last phrase of verse 15, which says, "Whoever reads, let him understand." The Jewish people who will be frantically searching for answers during the last days will read these words of Jesus and, hopefully, they will heed them. If not, they will fall for the deception that seeks to destroy them. In fact, Jesus's words in verse 26 indicate that attempts will be made to lure or entice the Jewish people to come out of hiding. They will be told that the Messiah is out in the desert or in a building somewhere, and if they leave their hiding, they will walk right into an ambush to be slaughtered. Jesus cautioned, "Do not believe it." Don't believe it because the true Messiah isn't going to be tucked away in a building somewhere, and he is not going to be hanging out in the desert. Instead, He will come in a blazing display of glory when He returns. His appearance will be clearly evident to everyone as the lightening comes from the east and flashes to the west. His coming will be public, visible, and universal. It won't be something that is subtle. Jesus emphasized this point by saying, "For wherever the carcass is, there the eagles will be gathered together" (Matthew 24:28). Even from a long way away, you can tell where a carcass is because of the circling birds above. In the same way, when the Messiah appears, it will be something that is seen and obvious, not something that is hidden and subtle. That's the point Jesus emphasized with both of His illustrations.

It is also possible that Jesus used the second illustration about the carcass and the birds to indicate that there will be a severe judgment when He returns. Revelation 19:17 records an angel issuing an invitation to the birds of the air to gather together for the supper of the great God and that invitation is in anticipation of the second coming of Christ.

It's fascinating to note that even during this present day there are so many birds which migrate directly over Israel that it's a problem for both commercial and military flights in and around Israel. The birds fly over Israel instead of over the Mediterranean Sea because they need to eat during the migration. And they fly over Israel instead of flying over the countries to the east of Israel because Israel is far more fertile than the desert countries to the east. So, when the angel calls together all the birds, it won't be a new location for many of them. They already go back and forth over that land, so they know it well.

So, both Jesus and John connected a feast of carnage with the second coming. Jesus will return to this earth someday. All the rebels gathered for the battle (Revelation 19) will be slain, and the birds will begin to consume their bodies. That is what will take place immediately after the tribulation. The darkness of those days will be followed by a blazing light.

9

The Sign of the Son of Man

Matthew 24:29–31

It would not be an exaggeration to say that one of the greatest minds ever to live was Saul of Tarsus, who is better known to us as the Apostle Paul. To use an expression, he had a mind *like a steel trap*. He could think as accurately, technically, deeply, and profoundly as any man ever. After he had contemplated and partially delineated God's fathomless plan of salvation, as set forth in the book of Romans, he uttered this lofty doxology in Romans 11:33-34: "Oh, the depth of the riches both of the wisdom and knowledge of God! How unsearchable are His judgments and His ways past finding out! 'For who has known the mind of the LORD? Or who has become His counselor?'" That is the proper response to a contemplation of God's plan to save the lost. The wisdom and knowledge displayed in God's plan is unfathomable.

The story of the Bible begins in Genesis 12. Why do I say that the story begins in chapter 12 of Genesis? Doesn't the story of the Bible begin in Genesis chapter 1? Yes and no. The first eleven chapters of Genesis tell us about 4 major events that are the key to understanding the rest of the Bible and all of life. Those four events are: creation, the fall, the flood, and the Tower of Babel. If you don't know about those four events, then you will never be able to answer questions about life.

Where did this universe come from? How did all of this get here? The answer: creation. "In the beginning, God created the heavens and the earth" (Genesis 1:1). The flowers, trees, lakes, rivers, oceans, and animals were all made by God. Then God used the dust of the ground to make the pinnacle of his creation—the human race.

But if God created everything, including man, and God is good, then how did this world get so messed up? The answer to that question is the fall of mankind into sin. Genesis 3 tells us about the most horrible event in all of history when Adam and Eve sinned against God and plunged humanity into sin. Because of sin, this wonderful world that God created is under a curse. That's why there are earthquakes, hurricanes, tornadoes, and other natural disasters. This world is out of sync because of the curse of sin. And that's our problem, too. The reason society and our world are so messed up is because of sin. The reason relationships are so messed up is because of sin. Understanding the fall of humanity into sin answers a whole host of questions.

The next major event in the book of Genesis is the flood. Because the wickedness of the human race grew so great and because of God's hatred for sin, He judged the entire world by sending a worldwide flood to destroy every living thing on the face of the earth, except for the people and animals that were in the ark. This helps us understand so many things about present-day geology like fossils, rock strata, etc.

The fourth major event in the first eleven chapters of Genesis is the Tower of Babel. Because mankind refused to obey God's command to scatter throughout the earth, God confused their speech by establishing different languages, and the result was that the people broke up into groups according to their language.

So, these four events—creation, fall, flood, and Tower of Babel—are foundational to understanding all of life and the rest of the story of the Bible. When you read about these events in the first eleven chapters of Genesis, you get the impression that the author is hurrying somewhat to get to chapter 12 because the actual story of the Bible begins in Genesis chapter 12 when God chose to begin carrying out His plan through a man named Abram, who later became Abraham. Chapters 1–11 cover hundreds and hundreds of years and include many different people, but the story slows down exceedingly when we come to chapter 12 and the camera zooms in on one man.

In Genesis 12, God began His plan by calling Abraham. We know from Joshua 24:2 that Abram's father was an idolater, worshiping other gods. Maybe Abram himself was an idol worshiper. So, why did God call him? Two words: sovereign grace. God was not obligated to save and bless Abram. In fact, God is not obligated to save and bless anyone. The only thing God owes the entire human race is the lake of fire. But, God is a god of grace, and He sovereignly chooses to bestow His grace upon undeserving mankind. That's what we see in the call of Abraham.

In Genesis 15, God established His covenant with Abraham. It's probably impossible to overemphasize the importance of that event. When God passed between the pieces of the animals alone, it was His way of promising that He would fulfill His covenant regardless of the faithfulness of Abraham or his descendants. In other words, it is an unconditional covenant in its ultimate fulfillment. It was conditional in the sense that to enjoy its benefits, it is necessary for the participants to have faith and obedience. But, it is an unconditional covenant in its ultimate fulfillment.

The Abrahamic covenant involves three components: a land, descendants, and blessings. God promised Abraham that he would have many descendants and that his descendants would possess the land of Canaan and that through his descendants God would bless the nations. That is the beginning of God's plan to save and bless the world. God has always had a heart for the world, and He has always had the perfect plan to bless the families of the earth, even though we might not be able to see it when God was focusing His plan on one man. That is not the way we would do it, but God's ways are so much higher and so much better than ours. As we read earlier from the pen of Paul in Romans 11:34, "Who has known the mind of the Lord? Or who has become His counselor?"

So God chose to carry out His plan through Abraham's descendants, the Jewish people. He didn't choose them because they deserve it, because they are better than other people, or because they are worthy; He chose them because of His sovereign grace. He chose them to be the people through whom the Scriptures and the Messiah would come and through whom He would bless the world. He chose them to be the people to whom He would eventually give the promised kingdom. God chose them and committed

Himself to them regardless. He made an unconditional covenant with Abraham to signify that unconditional commitment. That doesn't mean that He is going to take them into heaven apart from repentance and faith, but it does mean that the day will come when He will do what is necessary to bring them to repentance and faith. It will take the horrors of the future tribulation period and the second coming of the Lord Jesus to accomplish that. But it will certainly happen because Romans 11:29 says, "For the gifts and calling of God are irrevocable." God called Israel into existence and He bestowed on them numerous gifts, so it is certain that He will fulfill His promises. That commitment is what's behind Jesus's teaching in Matthew 24.

Jesus taught that He will return to this earth immediately after the tribulation of those days (Matthew 24:29). The tribulation will be so severe that unless those days were shortened, no flesh would be saved (Matthew 24:22). It is going to take supernatural intervention for the Jewish people to survive the Antichrist's attempts at annihilation. But they will survive. They will not only be saved physically, they will be saved spiritually because they will finally be brought to repentance and faith. All that will culminate with the second coming of our Lord Jesus Christ to this earth to end this present age and to usher in the promised kingdom. That is the focus of Jesus's words in verses 29–31.

When it is time for Jesus to come in blazing glory and splendor, God is going to turn out all the lights in heaven to get the world's attention and to provide a black backdrop for the glorious appearing that is about to take place. "The sun will be darkened, and the moon will not give its light" and even "the stars will fall from heaven" (v. 29). In addition to all this, there is going to be a massive heaven-quake.

A heaven-quake is like a violent earthquake, but it takes place in the sky. The powers of the heavens will be shaken. All this commotion will naturally direct people's attention to the sky. When God turns out all the lights and shakes the heavens, people are going to be focusing their attention on the sky to see what is happening. And that is exactly what God wants because God wants everyone to see what is going to happen next. Jesus is going to come in blazing glory and splendor.

The phrase "the sign of the Son of Man" in Matthew 24:30 doesn't refer to something else in addition to Jesus Himself. The sign is Jesus Himself. This phrase could be translated, "the sign, which is the Son of Man." The coming of Jesus in majesty and magnificence is the sign that this present age has come to an end, and He is about to usher in the next age, which is the kingdom age. This is such a significant event that God is going to make sure that no one misses it. "All the tribes of the earth... will see the Son of Man coming on the clouds of heaven with power and great glory." To say that it will be a spectacular sight would be a gross understatement. There is a sense in which it is beyond description.

When Jesus comes, it will be in glory, splendor, majesty, and brilliance. And all will see Him. What will be the response? Jesus said, "All the tribes of the earth will mourn." When Jesus returns to this earth, the vast majority of the people on it will not love Him. The book of Revelation makes that clear. People will be clenching their fists at the Lord during the tribulation period, and they won't be glad to see Him when He arrives. Unbelievers who are alive during the tribulation period will know that this earth is experiencing divine judgment but it won't bring them to repentance. Revelation 16:9 says, "They blasphemed the name of God." Revelation 16:11 says, "They blasphemed the God of heaven because of their pains." Revelation 16:21 says, "Men blasphemed God because of the plague of the hail." That will be the attitude of many people on the earth during the tribulation period. So it's no wonder that they will mourn when they see Jesus coming on the clouds. They will mourn the fact that He is going to win and not their leader, the Antichrist.

But there will be another kind of mourning from another group of people. The unbelievers are going to mourn the fact that they and their leader are defeated, but the people of Israel will mourn in repentance because they will realize that Jesus is their Messiah. The people of Israel will look on the One they pierced and "they will mourn for Him as one mourns for his only son, and grieve for Him as one grieves for a firstborn" (Zechariah 12:10). That is when they will be saved.

Jesus said that, at that time, "He will send His angels with a great sound of a trumpet, and they will gather together His elect from the four winds, from one end of heaven to the other" (v. 31). All the elect will be gathered together from heaven and earth because this will be the inauguration of the promised kingdom. It will be the culmination of the present age. But the sad fact is that there will be many people on planet earth at the time who are not ready for the Lord's return. Thus, Jesus used a significant portion of the Olivet Discourse to appeal to people to be ready.

10

Exhortations for Readiness

Matthew 24:32–35

History has been filled with some amazing events. Even in recent years we have seen some of the most astonishing events ever to happen. For example, we have all heard of the sinking of the supposedly unsinkable ship Titanic; we witnessed the horror of 9/11; and we have seen the almost unbelievable devastation caused by the tsunami that hit Southeast Asia when the Indian Ocean came ashore on December 26, 2004. Those were remarkable events in any era, and there have been others in recent times. Maybe you can still remember what you felt like when you saw the news coverage of the Berlin Wall coming down in Germany. Many people assumed they would never see that in their lifetime. So, history has been filled with some amazing events but all of them pale in comparison to one event that is coming in the future. It is the event to which all of human history is pointing. It is the second coming of our Lord and Savior Jesus Christ to planet earth.

Jesus gave His disciples much information about that future event, in response to their questions about the sign of His coming and the end of the age. But Jesus didn't stop there. After giving all the details about the future tribulation and His second coming, Jesus went on to draw some practical applications and implications from what He had taught. When the Lord tells about the future, He doesn't do so just to satisfy our curiosity. There are always practical applications and exhortations connected to the predictions. That's what is recorded in 24:32–25:30 of the Olivet Discourse. Jesus gave exhortations for readiness to those who will be living during that time.

The first one is in the form of a parable about a fig tree. That was an illustration the disciples and the first-century readers would have easily understood. Fig trees were abundant in the land of Israel and still are. Therefore, even in the future, when the Jewish people living in the land of Israel read these words, they will know what Jesus is saying. When the branch of a fig tree *puts forth leaves*, that means summer is near. In the same way, when people begin to see all the things that Jesus described back in verses 4–15 of Matthew 24, they should know that His return is very soon. When there is massive, worldwide death from war, famines, pestilences, and earthquakes in various places, that will be an indication that the birth pains have begun. When the abomination of desolation takes place, that will mean that the Lord's coming is even closer. As Jesus said, "Know that it is near–at the doors." In fact, Jesus said that the generation alive when all these events begin "will by no means pass away till all these things take place" (v. 34). Those who are living when the events mentioned in verses 4–15 begin to take place will not pass away until everything is accomplished to end the present age and bring in the new age. God will not allow His chosen people, the Jewish people, to pass away without fulfilling what He promised to them. The words of Jesus assure us of that certainty. Jesus stated that His words are more lasting, unchangeable, and permanent than heaven and earth. This present heaven and earth will pass away some day, but the words of Jesus will never pass away. They are certain, sure, and unfailing.

In the Greek language of the New Testament, there are two different ways to say no or to negate something. The speaker or writer can use the little word *ou* or he can use the little word *ma* (long a). Both of those words mean no or not. Both of them were used by Jesus in His statement, "Heaven and earth will pass away, but My words will be no means pass away" (v. 35). That is a double negative in the Greek language, which is the strongest way to negate something. In English, it is poor grammar to use a double negative but in Greek it is the firmest way to express a negative or a negation. That is the construction Jesus used. It's as if Jesus was saying, "Heaven and earth will pass away, but My words will by no means, will never, ever, can't happen, not a chance, pass away." When Jesus says something is going to happen, it is going to happen. It doesn't matter if we can understand how it will happen or if we believe that it can happen, it will happen. It doesn't matter if we can explain it or not, it will happen. Heaven and earth will pass away some day. Second Peter 3:10 says, "But the day of the Lord will come as a thief in the night, in which the heavens will pass away with a great noise, and the elements will melt with fervent heat; both the earth and the works that are in it will be burned up." Heaven and earth will pass away to make way for the new heavens and new earth but the words of Jesus will never pass away or fail. All that Jesus taught in the Olivet Discourse is going to take place. And those who live as if it is not going to happen are going to be filled with a regret that is beyond description when they are taken by surprise.

11

As in the Days of Noah

Matthew 24:36–44

We live in a day of instant communication. When something happens somewhere around the world, we are able to see pictures of the event immediately or almost immediately. Sometimes we see live pictures and sometimes the pictures we see are taken right after the event has taken place. For example, although most people in the US live hundreds of miles from Louisiana, we were able to see the astonishing flood that decimated New Orleans back in 2005. When an earthquake hit northwestern Turkey in 1999, it killed over fourteen thousand people and rendered over two hundred thousand homeless. We saw the scenes of that devastation within minutes. On May 13, 2008, a massive earthquake hit China and it killed approximately ten thousand people, injuring thousands more. We saw footage of the immense damage within minutes. The tsunami in Southeast Asia that came ashore in 2004 killed over two hundred thirty thousand people. That's almost a quarter of a million people! And we saw the pictures in a matter of minutes. It's a remarkable day and age in which we live.

Another aspect that is fascinating about these kinds of scenarios is the fact that when these monumental events take place, the rest of the world goes right on living as if nothing happened. It is amazing how life goes on in some parts of the world when other parts of the world are experiencing catastrophic disasters. For some people, life virtually comes to a standstill. For others, it goes right on without missing a beat. According to Jesus's teaching in Matthew 24, that's the way it is going to be at the end of the age. The Bible tells us that, during the future tribulation period, there are going to be cataclysmic events taking place on this planet. The Jewish people in the land of Israel are going to face the most severe persecution they have ever faced. It will almost annihilate them. Other places in the world are going to experience colossal earthquakes, gargantuan hailstones, severe famine, widespread plagues, scorched-earth conditions, water turned to blood, and other extraordinary catastrophes. Yet, during this time, life will go on as normal for some people in the world. People are going to get married and continue with the normal, daily responsibilities and obligations of life. They won't even realize that all of the unprecedented events taking place on the planet are a sign and a prelude to the second coming of the Lord Jesus Christ to this earth. Amazingly, they will be totally caught by surprise when He returns. That was the purpose of Jesus's reference to "the days of Noah" in the Olivet Discourse.

Jesus warned, in verses 4–22 of Matthew 24, about a time of tribulation that will come upon this earth. It will be so severe that the only word one could use to describe it would be *unprecedented.* Immediately after that time, Jesus will return. All the events of the tribulation period are a prelude and a precursor to His coming. Therefore, the people who are here on planet earth and are willing to learn what Scripture says about the end of the age should know that the coming of Jesus is near, once they begin to see all these events unfold. Amazingly, however, there will be a lot of people who don't care. They won't be interested in His second coming. Much of the world wasn't interested in the first coming of Jesus, and many won't be interested in His second coming. All they will want to do is continue on with life as normal. As a result, they will be caught completely by surprise when Jesus returns and takes them away into judgment. If they had any interest in being right with God and being ready for the second coming of Jesus, they could easily read the signs of the times. All they would have to do is watch the news to see all that is taking place around the world and then read their Bibles to see what it means. Then they would know. But they won't have any desire to pay attention to what Scripture says about the events that lead up to the end of the age. Thus, they will be completely caught by surprise.

Jesus acknowledged that, at that time, He didn't know the day and hour of His return. During the time of His incarnation when He was here on the earth, He didn't always use His attributes of deity. Specifically, He didn't often access His omniscience. That's why He could say, in verse 36, that He didn't even know the day and hour of His return. No one can know the day or hour. However, Jesus did indicate that the events of the tribulation period will be a sign that His coming is near. Nevertheless, just because those events will indicate that His coming is near, no one will be able to give the exact day and hour.

Just as the people living in the days of Noah were unprepared for the sudden judgment of the flood, so will people of the tribulation period be unprepared for the sudden judgment of the second coming. During the days of Noah, the people of the earth were exceedingly wicked and that brought about a worldwide judgment. During the days of the end times, the people of the earth will be exceedingly wicked and that will result in a worldwide judgment. In the days of Noah, life was proceeding as usual for people, when they should have been keenly aware that judgment was coming. This was especially true for those who knew that Noah was building the ark. The act of him building a huge boat for one hundred and twenty years should have been an attention-getter but people ignored the sign and went on with life. That's what some people will do in the future tribulation period. The signs will be all around them but they won't pay any attention to the signs whatsoever. They will carry on with eating and drinking, marriages and banquets, and other activities of life. So the coming of Jesus in judgment will take them away, just like the flood did in Noah's day.

Jesus illustrated this by saying two men will be working in the field: one will be taken away in judgment and the other left. Two women will be grinding at the mill: one will be taken away in judgment and the other left. A lot of Christians use these verses to describe the rapture and they say that one will be taken into heaven and the other left behind. That interpretation ignores the context of what Jesus was saying. He is talking about judgment. The one who is taken is not taken into heaven but rather taken into judgment. This is made clear by noticing that the ones who were taken away in verse 39 were all the unbelievers who were taken away by the flood. The flood took them away in judgment. So the ones taken in verses 40–41 will be unbelievers taken away in judgment and the believers will remain here on the earth to enter the kingdom, which takes place after the second coming. Therefore, Jesus warned that there are going to be people who will be completely caught off guard when He returns to this earth at the end of the tribulation period.

Jesus concluded this paragraph with an exhortation for people to be ready. He used the illustration of a thief to make the point. If you know a thief is coming, you take the necessary steps to avoid the danger and the damage that will occur. In the same way, those who see that Jesus is coming in judgment ought to do what is necessary to avoid the danger and the eternal damage that will result. When Jesus comes back to this earth, He is coming in judgment. It's easy for us to forget that. We look forward to the time when Jesus will come in the clouds to gather us to Himself (1st Thessalonians 4:13–18) but that's a different issue than His second coming to the earth in judgment. The first thing Jesus is going to do when He comes back to this earth the second time is to carry out severe judgment. Revelation 19:11 says "in righteousness He judges and makes war." Second Thessalonians 1:8 says He is coming "in flaming fire taking vengeance on those who do not know God, and on those who do not obey the gospel of our Lord Jesus Christ." He came the first time as a lamb to save and He will come the second time as a lion to judge. That's why Jesus used the imagery of a thief. A thief does exceeding damage to those who are unprepared for his coming, and Jesus will unleash eternal damage to those who are unprepared for His coming. Jesus was warning about unpreparedness. He may come back sooner than people think, or He may delay longer than expected. If He comes back sooner than people think, it will be easy for many to be unprepared and not ready. If He delays longer than expected, the tendency is to assume that He is not coming for a long time or not at all. Both conditions are deadly. If Jesus comes sooner than anticipated and people are unprepared, they will find themselves swept away into judgment. If Jesus delays longer than expected and people put off the decision to get right with Him until a later date, they will find themselves swept away into judgment. So, Jesus says, "Therefore you also be ready" (v. 44). If you are not ready, the miscalculation is not trivial or minimal. It is eternal.

This passage is about being ready for the second coming of the Lord Jesus Christ to this earth at the end of the age, but its principles apply to us today. What is it that keeps people in our day from committing their lives to Christ? It is seldom a vehement opposition to the Lord Jesus and to the gospel. There is far less of that than there is of disinterested preoccupation. Life is full of all kinds of activities. People go through life eating and drinking, marrying and giving in marriage, and carrying out the activities of life. They are just too busy and disinterested to give time to think about their eternal destiny and their relationship with the Lord Jesus. For them, the call of the gospel is a nuisance or interference. That is what keeps them from committing their lives to Christ. They may not be antagonistic against the gospel, but they are too preoccupied with the mundane matters of life. People go to school and go to work and play. Life has so many opportunities and so many responsibilities that they never give any thought to their eternal destiny. Is that you?

12

The Evil Servant

Matthew 24:45–51

It is truly amazing how some people, many people, are completely unwilling to do anything about impending doom and tragedy. You hear stories about this on a regular basis. I remember the story about a gentleman who lived near Mount St. Helens. When the warnings began to be issued that the mountain was going to explode, he disregarded the warnings and ended up buried under tons of lava, silt, ash, and mud. There are dozens of stories very similar to that one that have taken place or continue to take place in our world. You often see this same kind of thing in the way some people handle finances. They charge endlessly, thinking that the bills will never come due or maybe they will just go away. And when they do come, they somehow think that ignoring them will solve the problem. Some people believe that if they ignore warnings, the problem goes away. Others think that if they choose not to believe the warning, it somehow makes it untrue. Our Lord knows that there are multitudes of people like that, which is why He gave not one, not two, not three, not four, but five warnings to men and women about the urgency of making sure that they are ready for His second coming and ready for their eternal destiny. Those five warnings are found in Matthew 24–25.

The third exhortation to readiness that Jesus gave in the Olivet Discourse was in the form of a story about two servants, one faithful and one evil. It has a different emphasis than the illustration Jesus presented just prior to it, which was of a thief coming in the night and catching people off guard. That is an exhortation to be prepared in case Jesus comes back sooner than expected. By contrast, the illustration about the two servants warns people about assuming He's not coming back, if He delays longer than expected. Both assumptions can result in deadly consequences. In fact, the consequences can be eternal. If someone thinks, "Jesus isn't going to come back soon, so I have a lot of time later in life to get right with Him," that person will be unprepared for eternity if Jesus were to come back sooner than expected. On the other hand, if someone thinks, "People have been talking about Jesus coming back for a long time and it hasn't happened and it isn't going to happen any time soon," that person could easily put off the urgency of getting right with God. In both cases, even though the thought process is a little different, the result is the same in that the person enters eternity completely unprepared. That's why Jesus issued His warnings at the end of Matthew 24 and on into chapter 25. It is eternally critical for men and women to be ready for the second coming of the Lord Jesus and ready for eternity. It really is a matter of life or death—eternal life or death.

By telling the story of two servants, Jesus used an illustration to which the people of His day could easily relate. Many of the households had servants. If they were reliable, trustworthy, and competent in their work, they were sometimes exalted to positions involving significant responsibility. They were placed in positions as stewards that managed money or other servants or some aspect of the family business.

Jesus told this story because there is a sense in which all people are servants of God in that all are accountable to Him for their lives. Not every human being is a child of God but all are accountable to God as servants. Life is a stewardship from God. God has entrusted to all of mankind a host of things: life, time, natural abilities, wealth, possessions, opportunities, etc. Those are granted by God as a trust. Therefore, every human being will give an account to God someday regarding his stewardship. Some people take advantage of their opportunities to hear God's truth and respond to God's truth, others don't. Some people recognize that their lives are only temporary, so they prepare for eternity. Others do not. Some people recognize that their time, wealth, abilities, and possessions are a gift from God, and that leads them to repentance. As Romans 2:4 says, "The goodness of God leads you to repentance." Other people enjoy all those gifts from God, but they never acknowledge Him as the source. So, the story that Jesus told is a picture of humanity as a whole. God is the good master, and people are servants who are accountable to Him for their lives. The faithful and wise servant is the one who acknowledges that God is the source of all that he has. He understands that he is answerable to God and is accountable to God. So, he submits his life to the Lord to be a willing servant, not merely an accountable servant. When Jesus returns, He will reward those willing servants who have known Him and loved Him and lived for Him. That depicts one segment of humanity.

The other segment is presented by the example of the evil servant. That is someone who is only a servant in name. He is not a true servant of God because he doesn't know Jesus personally as his own Lord and Savior, as demonstrated by his punishment in the end. But he is a servant in name and is accountable to the master. In the story, this servant made the assumption that his master would not come back soon and he acted on his assumption by being evil. With that illustration, Jesus is warning the person who believes He isn't going to come back for a long time or maybe not at all. That kind of perspective helps people ignore their wickedness and pacify their consciences. When people can convince themselves that there is no accountability for their actions, the sin nature runs rampant because external restraints aren't enough to hold it back. Or if they convince themselves that the accountability is so far out in the future that it's irrelevant, then the same kind of thing happens. This is what we see in society all around us.

People dismiss the idea of God and judgment in numerous ways. One way they do so is by talking themselves into this perspective from an intellectual standpoint. They embrace the theory of evolution because that's a convenient way to dismiss the fact that God is the creator and the one to whom we are accountable. Another way people do this is by filling their lives with so much activity that they don't even have time to consider if there is a God. All this activity isn't necessarily bad stuff; it's just so much stuff that there is no time for contemplation, consideration, or examination.

So they don't ever stop to consider the fact that there may be a God to whom we are accountable. Another way people do this is by numbing their minds and senses by constantly putting in alcohol and/or drugs, whether prescription or recreational. It is scary how many people in our world are numbed down by chemicals. When they are in that condition, it takes the edge off the conscience. Another way people do this is by filling their minds with so many other things to think about by constantly listening to music, watching television, reading the paper or magazines, renting movies, etc. This is the norm for our day. People have so many gadgets and so many ways to fill their minds that thinking could become a lost art. And it is especially tragic when people refuse to think about the reality of God, accountability, and judgment. The evil servant is the one who, in whatever way, has talked himself into believing that Jesus isn't coming back, and there won't be any accountability for his actions. As a result, he lives his life in a wicked manner. What a shock it is going to be when Jesus does return.

At the end of this story, Jesus stated that the master will return and mete out judgment. Those who are not prepared will be completely taken by surprise and they will be sent away from the master. Jesus said the evil servant will be cut in two, which was an Old Testament practice of severe judgment, and consigned to his punishment with the hypocrites. He is a hypocrite because he is not a true servant of God. He's only a servant in name, not in reality. Such people will taken away to judgment, where "there shall be weeping and gnashing of teeth" (v. 51). That is an appalling description but we dare not dismiss it. Those are the words of Jesus. The gnashing of the teeth may be a reference to pain or it may be a reference to seething anger, or it may be a reference to both. Those who end up in that place of judgment will only have themselves to blame because Jesus gave ample warning.

13

The Unprepared Virgins

Matthew 25:1–13

The fictitious, yet penetrating, story is told of someone who overheard a conversation between Satan and his evil spirits.

Satan asked his hosts, "Who'll go to earth and persuade men for me to accomplish the ruin of their souls? What message will you use? How will you say what you want to say so that men and women, boys and girls, will turn away from the things of God?"

One demon stepped forward to volunteer and he said, "I'll tell people that there's no heaven."

Satan frowned and replied, "That won't work. For too many centuries mankind has been told that there's a heaven and our enemy, God, has given the Christian a book that talks about heaven and tells that there will no longer be death, tears, sorrow, pain, affliction, or tragedy."

A second spirit glided forward and said, "I'll go and I'll tell them that there's no hell."

Again Satan responded, "That'll not do. The conscience of man, if nothing else, convinces man that someday there must be a day of reckoning in which men and women will come to terms with their lives. In fact, that book I mentioned has more to say about hell than it does heaven."

Satan paused and said, "I need someone who'll make an appeal to all classes, ages, and cultures, in all the countries around the planet."

A third spirit glided forward and volunteered to go. He said, "I won't tell people there's no hell. I won't tell them there's no heaven. I'll tell them there's no hurry."

Although we don't know that such an interchange ever took place between Satan and his hosts, the point of the story couldn't be truer. Satan loves people to believe that there's no hurry when it comes to responding to the gospel. "You've got time. Tomorrow. Later on, you can come to terms with your standing before God." Satan loves to use procrastination to keep men's souls captive.

As Jesus continued His Olivet Discourse on into Matthew 25, He related another story to illustrate the importance of people being prepared for His return and ready for eternity. It is called the "Parable of the Ten Virgins." It is the fourth of five exhortations to readiness. A major emphasis of this story is that those who are not ready will not be given a second chance.

Once again, Jesus used a story to which the Jewish people of the first century could easily relate. For us to appreciate the point of the illustration, we need to acquaint ourselves with the marriage customs of the first century. First was the betrothal period. When a man and a woman were betrothed, they were legally married at that point. It was more than just an engagement. They were actually married but they did not live together or come together in sexual union. The betrothal usually took place at the bride's home when the groom and his father went to the girl's house to negotiate the bride price. Once that transaction had taken place, the couple was betrothed. The groom would then go back to his father's house and begin preparing a place for his bride. That would take him several months. Once he had prepared a place, he would come back for his bride. However, she didn't know when that would occur. Therefore, the bride had to be ready all the time and so did her bridesmaids. The wedding officially began when the groom arrived at the bride's house. He would take his bride on a procession to the place he had prepared and in the procession that followed behind would be the bridesmaids. If the groom happened to come at night to take his bride, the bridesmaids needed to have oil lamps for light on the dark roads and paths of the countryside. In addition, the bridesmaids were responsible to make sure that they had olive oil on hand for when the festivities began to take place. That's what Jesus was referring to when He spoke of the ten virgins who took their lamps and went out to meet the bridegroom (v. 1).

In the story, we are told why some of them were wise and some of them were foolish. Basically, it boils down to the fact that five of them were prepared and five of them were not, which is the whole point of the story. Those who were ready were wise and those who were not ready were foolish.

It is breathtaking to see how often Jesus divided humanity right down the middle. When we look at the billions of people on this planet, we see people in a number of different categories. We see people in different countries, classes, races, cultures, and religions. And while there is great diversity among the human race, there is a sense in which all people fall into one of two categories. You are either prepared for eternity or you are not prepared.

In the story, five virgins did not take oil with them and five did. When you read that part of the parable, it seems so obvious that it was foolish for the five bridesmaids not to take oil with them. It begs the question: Why would you take an oil lamp with you for light without bringing any oil along? The same kind of question could be asked of humanity in general. Why would people not prepare for eternity? Why would people not be ready for the second coming of the Lord Jesus? That's why Jesus called them foolish.

Another detail mentioned in the parable is that the bridegroom was gone longer than they all had suspected. As a result, they began to slumber and sleep. Some slept in assurance because they were ready, while others slept in carelessness. The latter condition is exactly what has happened with humanity in general. Because Jesus has been away for a long time, people have forgotten about the fact that He is coming back or they have dismissed the idea altogether. Their spiritual senses have become dull. They have lost the sharp edge of alertness. But He is coming back again. Even though most people don't know that or have forgotten it or have completely dismissed the idea, Jesus is coming back. And it will be a shocking surprise for many people. In the story, the five foolish virgins were not ready when the groom arrived and they tried to come up with some way to overcome their lack of preparedness. But it was too late. The foolish virgins missed the wedding. The door was shut.

It is probably impossible for us to imagine the horror that will be present in people's hearts when they realize that it's too late to get ready to meet the Lord. All the tears and sorrow in the world won't change anything at that point. It will be too late. That was Jesus's sober warning in the parable of the ten virgins.

14

The Unprofitable Servant

Matthew 25:14–30

One of the things that never ceases to amaze is the incredible mercy and patience of God the Father. As Scripture repeatedly says, He is "ready to pardon, gracious and merciful, slow to anger, abundant in kindness" (Neh. 9:17). Psalm 145:8 says, "The LORD is gracious and full of compassion, slow to anger and great in mercy." Nahum 1:3 says, "The LORD is slow to anger and great in power." His patience is mind-boggling. It is staggering.

The Son's patience was just the same when He was here ministering on earth. People rejected Him, ignored Him, spurned Him, conspired against Him, mocked Him, and lied against Him, just to name a few of the things people did to Him. Yet, He not only exercised self-control, He went way beyond that to appeal to people to come to Him for forgiveness and eternal life. Right at the end of His life, maybe even two days before His crucifixion and even after the leaders of Jerusalem had repeatedly tried to trap Him, He said, "O Jerusalem, Jerusalem, the one who kills the prophets and stones those who are sent to her! How often I wanted to gather your children together, as a hen gathers her chicks under her wings, but you were not willing!" He still wanted them to come to Him. Not only that, even when Judas was betraying Him in the Garden of Gethsemane, Jesus went up to him and called him *friend*. His patience was indescribable. He warned and exhorted people to avoid judgment because He was incredibly long-suffering. This reality is seen as you examine the Olivet Discourse because it contains five illustrations to warn people to be ready for His second coming. The fifth one is the focus of this chapter.

The parable of the unprofitable servant makes a very similar point as the previous one but in a different way. The primary point of the previous story told by Jesus is that those who are not ready will not be given a second chance. They had their chance and they missed it. The primary point of this parable is the catastrophe of missed opportunity. The servants in this parable all had the opportunity to be true servants but, in the end, it was demonstrated that not everyone who claims to be a true servant really is a true servant. Some who claim to be servants are only servants in name.

The man traveling to a far country in this illustration is representative of the Lord Jesus Himself. This man called all the servants together and gave them talents. That is not referring to natural or God-given abilities. A talent was a measure of weight back in ancient times, somewhere between fifty-eight and eighty pounds. One servant was given five talents, one was given two, and another was given one. The first servant took the opportunity that was granted to him and did something with it. He made another five talents with the opportunity. He didn't ignore, waste, or squander the opportunity. The second servant did the same as the first. He didn't have the same opportunity as the first servant, but he took advantage of what was granted to him. The third servant did not. He was given a talent of silver and buried it. That was a large sum of money he buried! So, one of the points Jesus was emphasizing is that this man was entrusted with a tremendous opportunity. Even though he was only given one talent, it was a tremendous opportunity. But this man didn't do anything with it. He dug a hole in the ground and hid his Lord's money.

The reason why Jesus stated that the master came back after a long time is because He is making the point that, as a result of the length of time between His first and second coming, many people are going to assume that He isn't coming back. He is warning the person who believes He isn't going to come back for a long time, maybe not at all. He knows human nature; He knows how people think and reason. He knows that when people assume there isn't going to be any accountability that makes it very unlikely they will think about God and judgment and moral responsibility. But the master in this story did come back. He came back and settled accounts with them. In other words, when the Master comes back, there will be accountability.

The first servant was able to show that he had been faithful with the opportunity granted to him by the master. He had received five talents and he did something with them. He didn't ignore, disregard, neglect, or dismiss them. That's what so many people do with the opportunities given to them by the Lord to respond to Him. They brush them off and go on with life. Not the first servant. As a result, he was invited to enter into the joy of his lord because he had demonstrated that he was a genuine servant, not merely a servant in name.

The second servant had not been given as many talents, thus he didn't have as much opportunity as the previous servant. However, he took the opportunity that was granted to him and he responded to it. Therefore, he received the same commendation as the previous servant. He was also invited to enter into the joy of his lord.

The third servant depicts an unbeliever. His description of the master as hard, difficult, cruel, or harsh proved that he didn't really know the master. Sadly, that is the way many people view the Lord because they think He is unreasonable to require repentance or unreasonable to restrict salvation only to those who come through Him. But those who view the master as hard, difficult, cruel, or harsh don't really know the master. The third servant was afraid but not afraid enough to do what he should have done with the opportunity granted to him. There are a lot of people like this in the world. They have some level of fear of the Lord, but it's not enough to compel them to take the opportunity to repent and get right with Him. Instead, they try to bury the issue, just like this man buried his talent in the ground. That's why the master refers to this kind of man as wicked and lazy. This servant had opportunity but he disregarded it. Thus, he forfeited the potential for what could have been his when the master returned. Remember, Jesus told this parable to warn people who are not going to be ready for His second coming and will be unprepared. The result will be that they will end up excluded from the kingdom because they will be sent to the place where there will be weeping and gnashing of teeth. Oh what a foolish forfeit and trade it is when people refuse the opportunity they are given to be right with the Lord! The sense of regret they will feel is unimaginable.

15

The Sheep and Goats

Matthew 25:31–46

If you had to choose one verse of Scripture that has impacted your life more than any other, what would it be? If I had to pick one, it would be 2nd Timothy 2:15, which says, "Be diligent to present yourself approved to God, a worker who does not need to be ashamed, rightly dividing the word of truth." The opening exhortation of the verse says "study" or "be diligent" or "do your best," depending on what English translation you consult. There is a strong emphasis on diligence and labor. The second phrase says, "A worker who does not need to be ashamed." The clear implication of that phrase is that a worker ought to be ashamed if he doesn't study and do his best at rightly dividing the word of truth. It is a shameful thing to twist the word of God, misuse it, or be sloppy with it. The third phrase says, "Rightly dividing the word of truth" or, as it is in some translations, "accurately handling the word of truth." Again, there is a clear implication behind that statement. If we are exhorted to rightly divide the word of truth, then that means it is possible to wrongly divide the word of truth.

The reason for beginning the chapter this way is because this text is one that is often misunderstood, misinterpreted, and misused because it is taken out of the context of the Olivet Discourse. Matthew 24–25 is all about future events that will come to pass. Jesus taught about the future tribulation period, the abomination of desolation, the persecution of the Jewish people, and His second coming to the earth to establish His kingdom. Between the time He comes to this earth and the actual establishing of the kingdom, there is going to be a judgment of all the nations of the earth. That is what is described in these verses.

Jesus specifically stated that this judgment will take place when He returns to sit on the throne of His glory (v. 31). He said in Matthew 24:29 that He is going to return "to sit on the throne of His glory immediately after the tribulation." During the tribulation period, which is immediately prior to the second coming, there is going to be a massive persecution against the Jewish people. They will be hated by all nations, according to what Jesus stated in 24:9. They are going to be hated because they are Jewish and the Christ-hating world will know that Messiah Jesus was also Jewish. The Jews are Jesus's Jewish brethren. He is a Jewish messiah. He came the first time to the lost sheep of the house of Israel (Matthew 15:24). He was born in the Jewish nation of Israel, raised, ministered, died, rose from the dead, ascended to heaven from, and promised to return there. As a result, the Jewish people are going to be persecuted, mistreated, imprisoned, abused, and killed because the Antichrist, who is the one that will commit the abomination of desolation, is going to unleash all of his fury against them. The Antichrist will be the head of the one-world government that will be over all the earth. He and the false prophet will require everyone to take a mark on the back of their hand or on their forehead (Revelation 13). Those who refuse will not be able to buy and sell. In light of all this, who is going to be willing to assist or come to the aid of the Jewish people? Who is going to be willing to feed them or give them drink, visit them in the hospital or in prison, or clothe them or shelter them? Who is going to be willing to minister to Jesus's Jewish brethren? The answer: Only those who have come to faith in Christ during the tribulation. No one who is a part of the system will be willing to minister to the Jewish people. No one who has taken the mark of the beast will be willing to minister to the Jewish people. Only those who have come to faith in Christ during the tribulation will be willing to risk their lives to aid Jesus's Jewish brethren. That is crucial to keep in mind for a proper understanding of this passage.

Those who pull this text out of its time frame end up teaching some kind of salvation by works: salvation by virtue of prison ministry, salvation by virtue of hospital ministry, or something similar. That kind of view completely ignores the setting or time frame of these words of Jesus. This is not the Great White Throne Judgment, described in Revelation 20. This is the judgment of those who just came through the tribulation period. Those who minister to the Jewish people will prove that they are the ones who are truly followers of Jesus during that horrible time.

The people who are gathered before Jesus for this judgment are all the Gentiles who lived through the tribulation. They will be judged based upon how they related to the Jewish people during that time. Those who refuse to come to the aid of the Jewish people will prove that they don't belong to Jesus, and those who do come to the aid of the Jewish people will prove that they do belong to Jesus. It will be very easy to judge who is a sheep and who is a goat.

Jesus is going to divide all these people into two categories because some are going to be welcomed into the kingdom and some are going to be sent to the everlasting fire (v. 41). The next event after the second coming and this judgment is the kingdom. Throughout the Old Testament, God promised a literal, earthly kingdom. Hebrew Scripture is filled with descriptions of it and the book of Revelation adds one additional fact by telling us that it will last a thousand years. That's what Jesus referred to by His words "the kingdom, prepared for you from the foundation of the world" (v. 34). Those who come to Christ by faith during the tribulation period will be welcomed into the kingdom. Their actions in relation to the Jewish people will verify the genuineness of their faith. Their works will not save them, but their works will reveal that they are redeemed. The Gentiles who will be a part of the Antichrist's system will hate the Jewish people and refuse to minister to them. They will be sent away from the presence of the Lord and His kingdom, and they will be consigned to the everlasting fire.

Jesus clearly stated that hell was prepared for the devil and his angels (v. 41). God did not create hell for people but many will end up there because they rejected or refused the truth and loved darkness rather than light. That's not only true of those who will be living in the future tribulation period; it's also true of all people who will end up there. Even those who never hear a clear presentation of the gospel to be able to reject it will end up there. Not because they didn't respond to a gospel they never heard, but because they had no interest in knowing the true God and loving Him. Instead, they love their sin and error, and they love the god they have created in their minds. So, they will end up in a place that God originally intended only for the devil and his angels.

The word that is translated *everlasting* in the NKJV of verse 46 is the exact same Greek word that is translated *eternal* at the end of the verse. The NASB, ESV, and the NIV translate it consistently, which is important to do because the punishment spoken of here is the same as the life. Both are eternal or everlasting. There are some people, even Christians, who refuse to believe that the future punishment of the wicked is going to be eternal. Instead of believing what the Bible teaches, they come up with alternative views. They say that God is eventually going to change His mind and let people out of hell, or they teach that the people who are sent to hell will be consumed or annihilated, which means they won't suffer eternally. As unpleasant as it is to consider and as difficult as it is to accept, the word of God teaches that the punishment of the lost in hell is just as never-ending as the bliss of the saved in the presence of the Lord. Remember, these are the words of Jesus! This is not the teaching of someone whose motive is a sinful and selfish hatred or revenge. This is the teaching of the One who He is described in Matthew 12:20 as being so gentle that "A bruised reed He will not break, and smoking flax he will not quench." This is the teaching of the one who, in Matthew 11:29, said, "I am gentle and lowly in heart." Yet, He taught continually that the future destiny of the wicked is eternal, conscious torment in the lake of fire. That is beyond our ability to comprehend. But, just because we can't fathom this doesn't mean we have the right to throw it out, as so many have tried to do. Jesus taught that the fire will not be quenched and the people will not die. It's absolutely horrible. It's indescribable. It's worse than we can really imagine. Yet, men and women choose to go there.

The very last statement Jesus made in the Olivet Discourse is about the eternal destiny of the saved and the lost. He ended with a comment about eternal punishment and eternal life. When it's all said and done, that's what matters most. So, where are you? Are you a child of God, headed for eternity with the Lord, or are you lost and headed to the eternal dwelling place prepared for the devil and his angels? If you end up there, you cannot say that you were never warned.

Appendix: Study Questions

Chapter 1: The Destruction of the Temple

1. Who destroyed the New Testament temple and when?
2. What was the name of the general who led the army to destroy Jerusalem?
3. What were the two occasions in the New Testament when Jesus cried?
4. In your opinion, what is the significance of those two events when Jesus cried?

Chapter 2: The Olivet Discourse

1. What are the two schools of thought regarding the timing of the Olivet Discourse?
2. What prompted Jesus to give this extended discourse?

3. What is the evidence that Jesus is describing a future tribulation period?
4. What is the evidence that the focus of this discourse is the Jewish people?
5. What future key events does Jesus specifically mention in this discourse?

Chapter 3: The Beginning of Birth Pains

1. What large section of Scripture is parallel with the description of the tribulation in Matthew 24?
2. What passage of Scripture in the Old Testament indicates that this final phase of God's dealings with Israel will last seven years?
3. What event will be the starting point for this seven-year period?
4. What will happen at the midpoint of this seven-year period?

Chapter 4: Hated By All Nations

1. What is the key evidence that shows the Olivet Discourse is intended for people living in the future?
2. What were Israel's three key wars in the 1900s?
3. What other New Testament passage reveals the fact that Satan will try to annihilate the people of Israel?
4. What will God accomplish through this future horrific time?

Chapter 5: The Abomination that Causes Desolation

1. What key event took place in Jerusalem in AD 70?

2. What key event took place in Jerusalem in AD 638 and 691?
3. What passages of Scripture indicate that there will be another temple in Jerusalem someday?
4. What Old Testament passage did Jesus refer to when He mentioned the abomination of desolation?

Chapter 6: Then There Will Be Great Tribulation

1. What is the common title of the man who will commit the abomination of desolation?
2. What verse in the New Testament gives him that title?
3. What passages of Scripture describe him?
4. Look up those passages of Scripture and develop a list of characteristics given to us in those texts.

Chapter 7: Israel's Flight from Antichrist

1. Name the two men in history who have had character traits similar to the future Antichrist.
2. What three traits are stated about him in Daniel 7?
3. What does Jesus tell the Jewish people to do when they see the "abomination of desolation?"
4. What conditions does Jesus specifically mention that could cause Israel's fleeing to be difficult?

Chapter 8: Warnings about False Messiahs

1. What three words are used to describe the Antichrist's future miracles?
2. What verse in the New Testament uses those three terms?

3. What does this tell us about the possible source of some miracles today?
4. What are the two possible meanings of Jesus's statement, "For wherever the carcass is, there the eagles will be gathered together" in Matthew 24:28?

Chapter 9: The Sign of the Son of Man

1. According to this chapter, where does the story of the Bible begin?
2. What are the four foundational events of Genesis 1–11?
3. What are the three components of the Abrahamic covenant?
4. Jesus stated that His second coming to the earth will immediately follow what?

Chapter 10: Exhortations for Readiness

1. What was the first illustration Jesus gave to exhort people to be ready for His second coming?
2. What was the meaning of this first parable?
3. What did Jesus mean by his statement that "this generation will by no means pass away" in Matthew 24:34?
4. What grammatical construction does Jesus to state how certain it is that His words will not fail to come to pass?

Chapter 11: As in the Days of Noah

1. Why did Jesus say that He didn't know the day or hour of His return?

2. What are the parallels between the days of Noah and the days of the end times?
3. In Jesus's illustration of the two men working in the field and two women grinding at the mill, the ones who are taken are taken where?
4. The ones who are left remain on earth for what?

Chapter 12: The Evil Servant

1. How many illustrations did Jesus give in the Olivet Discourse to warn people to be ready for His second coming?
2. What is the difference between this third warning and the previous one about the thief coming in the night?
3. What are some of the ways people in our world dismiss the idea of God and future judgment?
4. What is the emphasis of Jesus's phrase, "weeping and gnashing of teeth," in Matthew 24:51?

Chapter 13: The Unprepared Virgins

1. What was the marriage process in 1st century Israel?
2. What is the primary point of this parable by Jesus?
3. Although there are many different kinds and categories of people in the world, Jesus divided humanity into how many categories?
4. What were those categories?

Chapter 14: The Unprofitable Servant

1. What is the difference in emphasis between this parable of Jesus and His previous parable of "The Unprepared Virgins" in 25:1–13?

2. What do the talents represent in this story?
3. What did the various servants do with the talents entrusted to them?
4. What is the evidence that indicates the third servant was only a servant in name, not a true child of God?

Chapter 15: The Sheep and Goats

1. Summarize the meaning of 2nd Timothy 2:15 in your own words.
2. What is the significance of this verse in relation to the meaning of the sheep and goat judgment?
3. When will this judgment take place?
4. Who will be gathered for this judgment?
5. What will be the evidence to show who is a believer and who is not?
6. What event is going to follow this judgment?
7. According to Jesus' words, hell was prepared for whom?
8. Are you ready for eternity?

CPSIA information can be obtained
at www.ICGtesting.com
Printed in the USA
FSOW03n1402240816
24076FS

9 781680 280692